Jerome Bixby's
The Man from
Earth

adapted by

Richard Schenkman

based on the original motion
picture screenplay written by
Jerome Bixby

SAMUEL
FRENCH
FOUNDED 1830
NEW YORK HOLLYWOOD LONDON TORONTO
SAMUELFRENCH.COM

IMPORTANT BILLING AND CREDIT REQUIREMENTS

"Jerome Bixby's The Man From Earth"
Motion Picture Production Credits

FALLING SKY ENTERTAINMENT
Presents

A Film By
RICHARD SCHENKMAN

JEROME BIXBY'S THE MAN FROM EARTH

Directed By
RICHARD SCHENKMAN

Written By
JEROME BIXBY

Produced By
RICHARD SCHENKMAN
ERIC D. WILKINSON

Executive Producers
EMERSON BIXBY
MARK PELLINGTON

Director of Photography
AFSHIN SHAHIDI

Production Designer
PRISCILLA ELLIOT

Editor
NEIL GRIEVE

Music Composed By
MARK HINTON STEWART

Casting by
ELISABETH JERESKI

Costume Designer
JILL KLIBER

Unit Production Manager/First Assistant Director
MICHAEL R. MELAMED

Second Assistant Director
DANIEL R. SUHART

Sound Supervisor
JAMEY SCOTT

Art Director
LAUREN RUGGERI

Co-Producer
ROBBIE BRYAN

Associate Producer
MICHAEL R. MELAMED

Line Producer
STEVEN ALEXANDER

2nd Second Assistant Director
CHAD STEINER

Cast
(in order of appearance)

John	DAVID LEE SMITH
Dan	TONY TODD
Harry	JOHN BILLINGSLEY
Edith	ELLEN CRAWFORD
Sandy	ANNIKA PETERSON
Art	WILLIAM KATT
Linda	ALEXIS THORPE
Gruber	RICHARD RIEHLE
Moving Man #1	STEVEN LITTLES
Moving man #2	CHASE SPRAGUE
Officer	ROBBIE BRYAN

CHARACTERS

JOHN OLDMAN – About 35, good looking, competent, easygoing history professor

DAN – 60-ish professor of anthropology; big, fit

HARRY – 50's professor of biology; stocky, likable

EDITH – 50's, art history professor; a hint of the spinster about her

SANDY – Late 20's; fiercely intelligent, but reticent

ART – 50's, but holding desperately onto youth; archeology professor

LINDA – Very pretty young student; wide-eyed, yet smart

WILL GRUBER – 75, large, mustachioed, bluff

MOVING MAN #1 – Burly, uniformed mover from "Charity Now"

MOVING MAN #2 – Another uniformed mover from "Charity Now"

PARAMEDIC – Uniformed EMS worker (can be played by a Moving Man)

COP – Young uniformed officer (can be played by a Moving Man)

SCENE

A cabin in the California desert.

TIME

The present.

ACT I

Scene 1

(SETTING: Low desert in California. Winter. Late afternoon. An expanse of tan dirt, dotted with cacti. A small cabin a distance from the road, a log fence, an irregular patch of lawn.)

(A pickup truck is parked nearby; in it and near it are boxes of various items, many books, utensils, clothing, etc.)

*(**NOTE:** Most of the action will take place inside the cabin, and some on the porch, but some will also occur in the yard and by the truck and so there should be a representation of the exterior, even if it is more stylized than realistic. Nearly everything will play out in real time. Over the course of the next eighty minutes or so, the sun will sink lower into the sky until finally darkness falls.)*

*(**AT RISE:** **JOHN OLDMAN**, wearing a sweater and jeans, lifts a box off the ground and hefts it into the bed of the truck.)*

*(**JOHN** picks up a snowboard, finds room for it in a box. This act exposes something that looks like a small van Gogh, leaning against another box.)*

*(We hear a car arrive O.S.; the door opens, closes. **JOHN** glances toward the sound…for a split-second, he looks impatient. He then waves at the visitor, **DAN**, who walks onstage wearing a warm winter jacket.)*

DAN. *(coming up)* You don't waste time.

JOHN. I try not to.

*(**JOHN** struggles to lift a heavy box of books onto the wagon's gate.)*

DAN. Give you a hand?

JOHN. Sure.

> (**DAN** *grabs the other end of the box, and it's done. We hear another car arrive O.S., accompanied by O.S. chatter as the passengers get out.*)
>
> (*The new arrivals are* **EDITH**, **HARRY**, *and* **SANDY**, *who doesn't look entirely happy.*)
>
> (*All wear warm garb, carrying plates of wrapped food. They are all somewhat upset with John.*)

HARRY. Would you like to tell us what the hell that was all about?

> (**JOHN**'*s eyes meet* **SANDY**'*s, and he looks away.*)

JOHN. I don't like good-bye's.

HARRY. Kind of the *point* of a goodbye party.

> (**SANDY**'*s eyes are on* **JOHN**. *She wants to say something, but doesn't. There's clearly something between them.*)

HARRY *(cont'd)* We went to a certain amount of trouble, John. You could have at least stayed a few minutes, eaten some of the food we so feverishly prepared.

JOHN. I apologize.

> (**HARRY** *wants an explanation, but decides to let it go.* **EDITH** *gives* **JOHN** *a hug.*)

EDITH. Why are you moving so quickly? You only resigned two days –

DAN. You got the history chair at Stanford!

JOHN. I wish.

> (**HARRY** *hefts the plates. Tries to lighten it up:*)

HARRY. Pork chops, tacos, tuna salad, and Pom. If we'd had time, we'd have done something more grandiose. Candlelight dinner at McDonald's, strippers…

JOHN. *(smiles)* Pork chops will do. Thanks.

DAN. Art'll be along, too. He's…talking to a student.

> (*All generally acknowledge what Art is really up to.*)

EDITH. *(changing the subject)* Is George taking over for you?

JOHN. Or Trimble. *(looks at* **SANDY***)* The Dean made up his mind yet?

SANDY. He hasn't called.

*(***EDITH** *has spotted the "Van Gogh." Stares, bends over for a closer look.)*

EDITH. My God! What is this? It looks like a van Gogh, but I've never seen it before!

DAN. It can't be an original.

JOHN. 'Course not. Just a gift.

EDITH. Still…it's a superb copy. Contemporaneous, I think. *(glances at* **JOHN***)* May I?

(Off **JOHN***'s nod, she picks up the painting reverently.)*

EDITH *(cont'd)* These are the same stretchers van Gogh used.

DAN. Hey, there's writing on the back, in French.

EDITH. *(reading)* "To my friend, Jacques Borne." I wonder who he was.

JOHN. Somebody he knew, I guess.

HARRY. That's a brilliant deduction.

*(***HARRY** *continues on into the house.)*

EDITH. Surely you'll have it looked at sometime. Appraised?

JOHN. Maybe sometime. I wouldn't be interested in money for it.

*(***JOHN** *has been putting stuff into the wagon.* **EDITH** *gives him the painting. He puts it carefully in, slams the tailgate.)*

JOHN *(cont'd)* That's about it, for now. Come on inside?

(They walk toward the porch. **EDITH** *looks back once. The Van Gogh.* **JOHN** *calls out to* **HARRY***:)*

JOHN *(cont'd)* Just put the stuff in the kitchen. Electricity's on, the gas is off.

(They enter the cabin. The room is barren of almost everything except furniture. Empty bookshelves, no pictures or knickknacks. A fire burns low in the fireplace.)

(People shed their jackets. **HARRY** *unpacks food in the kitchen.)*

(EDITH *moves toward the kitchen, joining* **HARRY.** **SANDY** *moves near the fire, gazes absentmindedly.)*

JOHN *(cont'd) (to others)* Get comfortable while you can. Furniture's going this afternoon.

DAN. It's been years since I sat on a floor. I've forgotten her name.

HARRY. It's good for the back.

EDITH. Can we do yoga exercises?

HARRY. That's even better.

*(***JOHN** *and* **DAN** *settle into chairs. A moment of silence.)*

DAN. So you're leaving good old We Teach U. Rather suddenly, you'll admit. Truth time. Is there a problem, John?

*(***JOHN** *shakes his head.)*

DAN *(cont'd)* You know we'd want to help.

JOHN. That's appreciated. But, no, there's no problem.

*(***SANDY***'s face shows concern, and a little resentment.)*

DAN. Well, I guess I'm plain curious. Where are you going?

*(***JOHN** *indicates that he doesn't know.)*

HARRY. *(still in kitchen)* You're giving up tenure?

DAN. – a decade of professorship, in line to chair the department, and you don't know where you're going? Now I *am* curious.

JOHN. Call it cabin fever. After a while my feet get itchy. I've done it before.

DAN. You're too young to have done it before.

EDITH. *(in kitchen)* And he hasn't aged a day in ten years!

Every woman on the faculty would give anything for his secret.

HARRY. *(in kitchen)* Is that what you're after!

EDITH. *(in kitchen)* Oh, Harry, you stop that!

(**SANDY** *has moved near a fine hunting bow, leaning by the door. A rack of arrows. Several packed boxes nearby. She leans over to pick it up. Tries the tension and winces.*)

SANDY. Whoa! Can you pull this?

DAN. What do you hunt?

JOHN. Deer, mostly. Up around Big Bear.

HARRY. What – ?

(**HARRY** *and* **EDITH** *return from the kitchen.*)

DAN. Some people can't bag a deer with a rifle and telescopic sight.

HARRY. With a *bow* and *arrow?*

DAN. Good eating.

JOHN. The best. Wild game. It eats naturally, lives naturally –

(**JOHN** *falls silent, hearing a motorcycle pulling up O.S. Opens the door, steps outside...*

The motorcycle is turned off and we hear O.S. chatter as two people remove their helmets and approach the cabin: **ART JENKINS**, *and* **LINDA**, *a student.*)

JOHN *(cont'd)* Art.

ART. John.

(*They shake hands.*)

You remember Linda? Had her last year. Now she's one of my victims. I'm...taking her home, she wanted to say hi and good-bye to you.

JOHN. Hi, Linda. Is Art as tough as I hear?

LINDA. Archeology's tough. Dr. Jenkins is a fine teacher.

(*As* **ART** *and* **LINDA** *enter the house:*)

ART. Very politic.

LINDA. Very true!

(As JOHN closes the door, ART hands him a book:)

ART. To read on the road.

JOHN. (reading) "Shadows of the Cave – Our Parallels to Early Man," by Arthur M. Jenkins. Thanks, Art.

ART. Publish or perish, eh?

JOHN. I'd certainly rather read than write another book.

ART. Where are you going? Like we care.

DAN. We've already covered that. He gets itchy feet.

HARRY. There are over-the-counter remedies for that.

(JOHN doesn't laugh.)

DAN. Then there is a problem?

JOHN. No. I just like to move on now and then. It's a personal thing.

DAN. Not to pry.

(A long, uncomfortable beat. JOHN has shut them all down. They wonder if they should leave…He suddenly warms:)

JOHN. Well, I can't offer you much, except seats for your behinds, and conversation. But I do have this!

(pulls out a bottle)

HARRY. Johnny Walker Blue? I didn't even know they made it in blue! What do they pay you?

JOHN. Nothing's too good for my friends. But we're down to paper cups.

DAN. A sacrilege I'll tolerate.

(JOHN pours whiskey for them. As he pours SANDY's cup, their eyes meet. Again, she wants to say something, but doesn't. JOHN starts to pour LINDA a cup, and she shakes her head.)

LINDA. Thanks, Dr. Oldman. I don't drink.

HARRY. We won't card you, sweetheart…

(Still, she demurs. Those with cups raise them.)

DAN. Long life and good fortune to our friend and colleague, John Oldman. May he find undeserved bliss, wherever he goes. Skoal!

(They drink.)

(Moment of silence. Now what?)

ART. Well, John, we're all sorry to see you go. Truly. Now what do we do with the rest of the afternoon?

HARRY. Anyone got a good topic?

*(**DAN** has been looking over the bow again. Now he spots something in one of the boxes nearby.)*

DAN. Like this, maybe.

*(**DAN** takes the item from the box, turns it over in his hand. **ART** glances over, then reacts with sharp interest.)*

ART. Hey, let me have a look at that!

SANDY. What is it?

DAN. A burin. Parrot beak, with inclined chisel point. I'd say probably Magdelanian.

*(**DAN** hands the object to **ART**, who inspects it carefully.)*

ART. Sure enough.

LINDA. What's a burin?

ART. A flint tool for grooving wood, bone – especially antlers – to make spear and harpoon points. The Magdelanians weren't noted for flint work. This is a nice specimen.

HARRY. Okay. What's a Magdelanian?

DAN. A later Cro Magnon, without getting technical. The final culture of the Upper Paleolithic. If stones could speak, eh? Where did you get it, John?

*(**JOHN** seems to rouse from introspection.)*

JOHN. Believe it or not, from a thrift shop. For a quarter.

ART. What a lucky bastard. *I* have to go digging for that kind of stuff!

HARRY. Can I look at it?

(JOHN *nods. The burin is passed around.* JOHN *is again looking thoughtful. Finally* LINDA *hands the burin to* JOHN, *who puts it back in the box. A moment of silence.*)

JOHN. Maybe – I'm glad you did this.

DAN. Did what? You mean, coming over? *(off John's nod)* "Maybe?"

JOHN. Definitely.

HARRY. Gee, thanks.

DAN. Well, so are we. So are we. We couldn't let you just run off.

JOHN. Thanks.

(*Another silent moment. Several puzzled expressions.*)

HARRY. What, are you on America's Most Wanted?

DAN. Out with it. You're among friends!

EDITH. Snoopy friends.

(JOHN *eyes are distant.*)

JOHN. Forget it.

HARRY. Confound it, John, you're *creating* a mystery! Obviously there's something you'd like to say. Say it!

JOHN. Yeah. Maybe.

(*Again he's silent.*)

HARRY. Ten, nine, eight, seven –

SANDY. – stop! –

JOHN. There is something I'm kind of tempted to tell you. I think. I've never done this before. I wonder how it would pan out.

(*An uncomfortable silence…where is this going?*)

JOHN *(cont'd)* Okay. To pass the time, I wonder if you'd answer a silly question for me.

ART. We're teachers. We answer silly questions all the time.

(*A look from* LINDA…)

JOHN. What if a man from the Upper Paleolithic had

survived until the present day?

HARRY. What does this have to do with –

DAN. You mean just, survived? Never died?

JOHN. Yeah. What do you think he would be like?

HARRY. *I've* met some guys. You ever been to the Ozarks?

DAN. It's an interesting idea. You working on a science-fiction story?

JOHN. Say I am. What do you think he would be like?

HARRY. Pretty tired?

DAN. Seriously? Well, okay. As Art's book title implies, he might be about like any of us.

EDITH. Dan – a caveman?

DAN. There's no anatomical difference between, say, a Cro Magnon and us.

ART. Except that as a rule we've grown a little taller.

LINDA. What's the selective advantage of height?

ART. The better to see predators in high grass, my dear.

DAN. Actually, tall and skinny radiates heat more effectively in warm climates.

ART. As for Neanderthals, we've all seen apish people. That strain is still with us.

EDITH. But he'd be a caveman.

DAN. No, he wouldn't. John's hypothetical man would have lived through about a hundred and forty centuries –

ART. – roughly –

DAN. – and changed with every one of them – assuming normal intelligence, and men of the Upper Paleolithic were, we think, quite as intelligent as we are. They just didn't know as much. But John's man would have learned as the race learned. In fact, if he had an inquiring mind, his knowledge might be astonishing. *(takes a sip)* If you do write it, let me have a look. You'd probably make anthropological boners.

JOHN. Deal.

LINDA. What would keep him alive?

EDITH. *(looks at* **HARRY***)* What does a biologist say?

HARRY. Cigarettes and ice cream. *(gets laughs)* Okay, okay, I'll play. In science-fiction terms, perfect regeneration of body cells, especially in vital organs. The human body appears designed to live maybe a hundred and ninety years. Most of us die of slow poisoning.

JOHN. Maybe he did something right. Something everybody else in history has done wrong.

ART. Like eat the food, drink the water, and breathe the air?

DAN. Prior to modern times, those were pristine. We've extended our life-span in a world not fit to live in.

HARRY. It could happen. The pancreas turns over cells every twenty-four hours, the stomach lining in three days, the entire body in seven years. But the process falters. Waste accumulates and eventually is fatal to function. If a quirk in his immune system led to perfect detox and renewal, he could duck decay.

EDITH. Now there's a secret we'd all like to have!

JOHN. Would you really want to do that? Live fourteen thousand years?

HARRY. *(the Gershwin tune:)* *"But who calls that livin', when no gal will give in, to no man who's nine-hundred years?"*

ART. If I was healthy, and didn't age, why not?

LINDA. What a chance to learn!

SANDY. *(changing the subject)* Anyone hungry?

(Off their affirmatives, **SANDY** *heads for the kitchen.)*

HARRY. The more I think about it, it's possible. Anything's possible. One century's magic is the next century's science. They thought Columbus was nuts. Pasteur, Copernicus…

JOHN. Aristarchus, long before that. I had a chance to sail with Columbus, but I'm not the adventurous type. I was pretty sure the world was round – but still, he might fall off an edge someplace.

(Silence.)

ART. Look around you. We just did.

(Silence.)

DAN. Well, I guess there's a joke in there somewhere, but I don't get it.

JOHN. Nothing to get.

DAN. What are we talking about? Explain.

JOHN. You did a pretty good job of that.

ART. We've been talking about a caveman who survived until this time.

JOHN. As you said, what a chance to learn. Once I learned to learn.

(Silence.)

DAN. Did you start the whiskey before we got here?

JOHN. Pretend it's science-fiction. Figure it out.

HARRY. A very old Cro Magnon, living until the present...

*(**JOHN** grunts loudly. Shockingly.)*

*(After a blank moment, **ART** starts to laugh. **DAN** and **HARRY** join in. **LINDA** is staring at **JOHN**. **SANDY** comes to the kitchen door.)*

SANDY. What's going on?

ART. John has confided that he's fourteen thousand years old!

SANDY. He doesn't look a day over nine hundred.

*(**SANDY** turns back into the kitchen. The chuckles subside.)*

ART. O-*kay.*

HARRY. *(Shatner imitation)* All right, Spock, I'll play your little game. What is it you want? What's the punchline?

JOHN. I have to move on every ten years or so, when people start wondering why I don't age.

ART. Very good. Quick. Let *me* see your story too, when it's done.

JOHN. Do you want more?

HARRY. By all means. This is great. So you think you're a Cro Magnon?

JOHN. Well, I didn't go to school and learn it. It's my best guess, based on archeological data, maps, anthropological research. Since Mesopotamia, I've got the last three or four thousand years straight.

ART. You're ahead of most people. Do go on.

(**DAN** *and* **ART** *are amused. But underneath, puzzlement is starting to show. What gives?*)

JOHN. You know all the background stuff, so I'll make it short. In what I call my first lifetime, I aged to about thirty-five or so, what you see. I ended up leading my group. They saw me as magical. I didn't even have to fight for it. But finally there was fear. They chased me away. They thought I was stealing their lives to stay young.

HARRY. The prehistoric origin of the vampire myth?

JOHN. The first thousand years I didn't know up from sideways.

DAN. How do you know, a thousand years?

JOHN. An informed guess. From what I've learned, and my memories.

ART. Most of us can scarcely remember our own childhoods, but you have memories of that time.

JOHN. Like yours. Selective, the high points. And traumas, they stick in the mind forever. A put-down at three or thirty, you still feel a twinge.

DAN. Go on.

JOHN. I kept getting chased because I didn't die. I got the hang of joining other groups I found. I also got the idea of moving on periodically. We were semi-nomadic, of course, following the weather, the game we hunted. Those few first thousand years were cold. We learned it was warmer at lower elevations. Late Glacial period, I guess.

ART. What was the terrain like?

JOHN. Mountainous, plains off to the west. Snow and ice.

DAN. West? Something you learned in school?

JOHN. Toward the setting sun. Another assumption based on memory. In fact, I suspect I saw the British Isles from what is now the French coast. Huge mountains in the distance, on the other side of an enormous deep valley, shadowed by the setting sun. Before they were separated from the continent by rising seas as glaciers melted.

HARRY. That happened?

DAN. The end of the Pleistocene. So far what he says fits.

(SANDY and EDITH have come to the kitchen door. A touch of concern in SANDY's eyes.)

ART. Into any textbook.

JOHN. That's where I found it! How can I have knowledgeable recall, when I didn't have knowledge? It's retrospected. All I can do is integrate my recollections with modern findings.

EDITH. A caveman! Are you going to hit me over the head with a club and drag me into the bedroom?

JOHN. You'd be more fun conscious.

EDITH. Oh, John.

(EDITH turns back into the kitchen. SANDY stays in the doorway.)

HARRY. Let's get one thing straight. We're not talking reincarnation. You're not saying you remember – what would it be? – maybe two hundred lifetimes. Dying and being born again.

JOHN. One lifetime.

HARRY. Some lifetime. Maybe there is something to reincarnation. You're supposed to come back again and again, and learn and learn. You just bypassed all the other bodies.

DAN. John, what is the point?

LINDA. *(ignoring* DAN*)* How about oceans?

JOHN. I didn't see any until much later.

LINDA. How would you know an ocean from a lake?

JOHN. Big waves. Something else I can surmise only in retrospect.

LINDA. Were you curious about where it all came from? The question of origin?

JOHN. We'd look at the sky and wonder. There had to be big guys up there. Otherwise, what made all this down here?

EDITH'S VOICE. *(from kitchen)* Shit!

(All suddenly look over –)

EDITH. I dropped the tuna salad.

(The rest now look back to JOHN*:)*

JOHN. At first I thought there was something wrong with me. I thought maybe I was a bad guy, for not dying. In my way, I wondered if I was cursed, or maybe blessed. Later on, I wondered if I had a mission.

EDITH. *(from kitchen door)* And now, do you think you do? God works in mysterious ways.

JOHN. I think I just happened.

*(*JOHN*'s cell phone rings, on a table. He goes to answer it. Others look after him, concerned.* EDITH *starts to bring out food.)*

JOHN *(cont'd) (into phone)* Hello? Yes, Elly. Harrison can't find your midterm? Hold on. Sandy?

*(*SANDY *digs into her briefcase. Pulls out papers. She brings them over to* JOHN*.)*

SANDY. Sorry. I picked it up by accident, with the periodicals.

JOHN. Got it. What was that? *(listens)* Oh. You're worried about your parents.

*(*JOHN *casually riffs the papers as you would the corner of a deck of cards. Finds Elly's: it's a D.)*

JOHN *(cont'd) (into phone)* Don't worry, you passed. C plus. I'll make sure it gets back to the office…You're welcome. *(hangs up)* Nice kid. What does a pre-med need with history? *(gives papers to* **SANDY***)* Make it so.

*(***SANDY*** *sits, balancing the papers on a knee, and starts to edit Elly's test to C plus.)*

(The others are eating, drinking beers.)

LINDA. More.

ART. I was hoping we'd left that behind.

HARRY. Oh, let's go with it, Art, it's interesting! And he's making some sense, you know.

ART. Like Hegel. Logic from absurd premises.

(Over the following, they they continue eating and drinking.)

EDITH. That van Gogh.

JOHN. He gave it to me. I was Jacques Borne at the time, a pig farmer.

(The others laugh: "pig farmer!")

JOHN *(cont'd)* I like to work with my hands. He'd come out to my place and paint. We would talk about capturing Nature in art. Turner, Cezanne…

EDITH. The Nolde landscapes.

JOHN. Not in van Gogh's time.

(as **EDITH** *is embarrassed)*

He would have liked them, though.

LINDA. I can't understand why you don't know where you were, back then. The geography hasn't changed. I learned that in –

ART. *(cutting in)* Professor Hanson's tepid lectures. But you're right.

*(***LINDA*** *shoots* **ART** *a look; he places a hand on her arm, a bit condescendingly, and she pulls away.)*

JOHN. *(to* **LINDA***)* Where did you live when you were five years old?

LINDA. Little Rock.

JOHN. Your mother took you to the market. *(off LINDA's nod)* Which direction was it. I mean, from your house?

LINDA. I don't know.

JOHN. How far?

LINDA. About three blocks.

JOHN. Do you remember anything you saw on the way there? Any reference points that stuck?

LINDA. There was, I think it was a gas station. And a big field. I was told never to go there alone.

JOHN. If you went back there now, would it be the same?

LINDA. Oh, no, I'm sure it must be all different now. Built up...

(She falls silent, getting the point.)

JOHN. Like the saying, you can't go home again, because it isn't there anymore. You've had the experience, picture it on my scale. I migrated through an endless flat place with endless new things. Forests, mountains, rivers, tundra. My memory sees what I saw then; my eye sees freeways, urban sprawl, Big Macs under the Eiffel tower. Early on, the world just got bigger and bigger, and then...Think what I've had to unlearn.

(Silence. Digesting, skeptical, curious faces.)

ART. Now you're moving on again.

JOHN. As Edith said, there's talk about my not aging. When that happens, I'm gone.

DAN. It might make sense to set up your next identity, your next ten years, and then just drop into it.

JOHN. I've done that. I've even passed as my own son. "Oh, you're an engineer too? Well, Ben was a good man. You're hired." Saves trouble with credentials, references. On the other hand, I've been busted a few times. I spent a year in jail in Belgium, 1862. That's a date I remember, for faking a government application.

LINDA. When did you come to America?

JOHN. 1890, right after van Gogh's death. With some French immigrants. Moving on.

ART. An answer for every question, except one. Why are you doing this?

JOHN. A whim. Maybe not such a good idea. As I said, it's a first. I wanted you to say good-bye to me, not to what you've thought I was.

ART. Since this isn't funny, we think you may be having a problem. A serious problem.

JOHN. Hmm. Well, I'm going to lug some boxes.

(ART *rises, crosses to the farthest corner, pulls out his cell phone.* JOHN *bends to pick up a box beside the door.*)

SANDY. I'll help.

(DAN *leans over and fingers the burin in the box* JOHN *is holding.*)

DAN. Wouldn't you have relics, artifacts, of your early life? This, maybe?

JOHN. Thrift shop. Really.

(*He takes a pen from the box.*)

If you lived a hundred, a thousand years, would you still have this? As a memento of your beginnings? Even if you didn't have the concept of beginnings? What would have caused you to keep it? It would be lost. It might not exist any more. No, I don't have artifacts.

DAN. Interesting. You could have lied about that.

JOHN. Don't talk about me while I'm gone.

(JOHN *and* SANDY *go out the front door, with boxes and the bow in its closed case, head for the truck.*)

(*Back inside the house, out of earshot:*)

DAN. Is he serious?

EDITH. If so, I'm sorry to say, he's...How could he have concealed that for ten years?

HARRY. Well, at least he doesn't appear to be dangerous.

(HARRY *is ostentatiously looking around. Pokes into the*

cushions of his chair.)

DAN. What are you doing?

HARRY. Looking for a hidden mike.

(**ART** *continues to speak quietly into his cell phone, then ends the call and puts it away. He rejoins the others.)*

(*Stage lighting moves the focus from the guests inside the cabin to* **JOHN** *and* **SANDY** *at the truck. They are fitting boxes into the wagon. A slight breeze has whipped up. A distant haze of dust reddens the low sun.)*

SANDY. I love you, you know. *(off his gentle look)* Since my first week at the office.

JOHN. I know.

SANDY. And?

JOHN. I care very much about you. But now you know what you'd be getting into.

SANDY. Do you really believe you're a caveman?

JOHN. Do you?

(**SANDY** *studies his expression. After a long beat:)*

SANDY. Could you love me? Or you don't believe in it any more?

JOHN. I've gotten over it too many times. I enjoy companionship, and I'm fond of you. Certainly attracted.

SANDY. That's it? *(beat)* I can work with that.

JOHN. If what I'm saying is true, you and any children will age. I won't. And one day I'll leave.

(*She looks at him, trying to hassle it in her mind.)*

SANDY. Talk about your May-December romances.

JOHN. *(a sad smile)* The simple fact is, I can't give you forever.

SANDY. How long is forever? Who ever really has it? My parents split up before I was born! Mom's next marriage lasted a whole three years. And then there's illness and death and acts of God. *(off John's silence)* No one knows how long they have. Or how little. *(takes his hand)* I love you. And I'll take whatever you can give.

JOHN. *(soft – blunt)* Like ten years?

> *(After a few moments, they cross back to the house.)*

> *(As JOHN and SANDY enter: HARRY waiting is near the door. HARRY grabs JOHN around arms and waist.)*

> *(A flash of action, and HARRY is on the floor, flat on his back, John's knee on his chest, their faces inches apart. Others react. SANDY has pressed herself against a wall.)*

JOHN *(cont'd)* Why did you do that?

HARRY. I wanted to see how fast you are. Test your reflexes.

JOHN. I don't have eyes in the back of my head. I can't hear a flea breathing. I am not, in any way, Superman.

HARRY. I'm a second-degree black belt!

JOHN. Give it another thousand years.

> *(JOHN tries to help HARRY to his feet; HARRY waves him away.)*

DAN. Smooth demonstration, Harry.

HARRY. Sit on it, Dan.

ART. *(quietly, to HARRY)* Still think he's not dangerous?

> *(SANDY is disturbed by the darkening tone.)*

SANDY. Guys, please.

LINDA. Well *I* still have questions.

ART. *(baiting JOHN)* Yeah, so do I. Are we through with pre-history yet? Do you remember any of your original language?

> *(JOHN looks to SANDY for a cue… "should I?" She nods.)*

JOHN. A little. One thing that hasn't changed much.

> *(He gestures with his head, making a wolf-whistle toward SANDY. Some laughs…)*

LINDA. Did you ever do any cave art?

JOHN. You've seen the rock art at Les Eyzies? Some of them were the work of – what was his name? – Gurar. He was pretty good at it. He'd draw the animals we hoped to find, eat. One time after a fruitless hunt, our chief stomped his teeth out. His magic had failed. After that, somebody had to chew his food for him. Finally he got, I suppose, an infected jaw. He was abandoned.

EDITH. That's awful.

LINDA. Is all this why your students say your knowledge of history is so amazing?

(**ART** *gives her an impatient look.*)

JOHN. No, that's mostly from study. Again, it was always one man, one place at a time. My solitary viewpoint, in a world I knew almost nothing about.

DAN. Let's talk about what you say you do know about. Historical times.

EDITH. Oh, don't encourage him!

JOHN. Over the next few thousand years, the Neolithic, it got warmer.

ART. 'A few thousand years.' I *know* you're guessing.

JOHN. You can't get there from here.

ART. Pray continue.

JOHN. We hunted reindeer, mammoth –

ART. …bison, horses. Then game retreated northward as the climate changed. You got the idea of growing food instead of gathering it, raising animals instead of hunting them. Am I getting warm? Lakeside living became the norm. Fishing, fowling. Again, out of any textbook.

JOHN. Even yours. You had most of it right. Finally I headed east. I'd become curious about the world, wanted to explore. I'd gotten the hang of going it alone, and fitting in when I wanted to.

DAN. East, toward the rising sun.

JOHN. I thought it might be warmer over there. That's when I saw an ocean. The Mediterranean, probably. This was around the beginning of the Bronze Age. I followed trade routes from the east, copper, tin, learning languages as I went. And everywhere creation myths, new gods, so many and so different I finally realized they were probably all hogwash, though it was wise to pretend belief. I was Sumerian for maybe two thousand years, then Babylonian…finally under Hammurabi, a great man. Then I sailed as a Phoenician for a time. Moving on had been easy as a hunter-gatherer, harder when villages emerged, tougher still in city-states where authority was centralized and strangers were suspect. It seemed like I was always on the move. I learned some tricks. Even faked my death a few times. I headed east again, finally to India, luckily at the time of the Buddha.

ART. Luckily?

JOHN. The most extraordinary man I've ever known. He taught me things that I'd never thought about before.

HARRY. You studied with the Buddha?

JOHN. Until he died. He knew there was something special about me. I never told him.

DAN. Well, it sounds fascinating. I almost wish it were true.

ART. If it is true, why are you telling us? We might tell others.

JOHN. *(shrugs)* It would vanish in disbelief. The story that goes around the room, no credibility. If I could make any of you believe me, in a month you wouldn't. Some of you would say I'm a psychopath, others would be angry at a pointless joke.

ART. Some of us are angry now.

JOHN. I guess this was a bad idea. I love you all, I don't want to put you through anything. I'm sorry if I have.

EDITH. Then why are you doing it!

JOHN. I wanted to say good-bye –

EDITH. *(cutting in, cold)* As "yourself." Well, I'd say you've done that. Whatever that "self" is.

DAN. Easy, Edith, we're just grading his homework.

ART. *(to DAN)* You're playing good cop. Enjoy it. This is a crock, and I'm tempted to walk out –

JOHN. I'm sorry. I don't like to hurt anyone.

ART. – but I won't. I'm curious. I want to know what the hell this is about.

EDITH. I agree, John! What is this all about?

(*Under above, sound of a car pulling up outside.* JOHN *glances out the window. His expression turns wry.* ART *rises –*)

ART. And here comes Dr. Freud.

(*Footsteps on the porch.* ART *opens the door, revealing* WILLIAM GRUBER.)

GRUBER. John! I'm glad I caught you! Someone mentioned you were leaving today –

JOHN. (*cutting in*) – someone called you and told you I've lost it. Come on in, Will. This is going in unexpected directions.

GRUBER. (*entering*) So I hear.

(GRUBER *nods to the others.* SANDY *indicates the paper plates.*)

SANDY. Are you hungry? Pork chop, taco, cake?

GRUBER. Ah. Thank you, no.

JOHN. Whiskey?

HARRY. Johnnie Walker Blue!

GRUBER. Oh, yes!

(JOHN *pours a cup for* GRUBER, *who glances at* ART *and* LINDA, *instantly sizing up the situation.*)

GRUBER (*cont'd*) (*to* LINDA) You look familiar, my dear.

LINDA. Linda Murphy. I'm in your Tuesday Psych One class.

GRUBER. Well, this may be a lesson I could not have imagined. (*to* JOHN) I regret being obvious, John. These people are concerned for you.

JOHN. Yeah, I'm cutting out paper dinosaurs.

GRUBER. I really wish I'd been here at the beginning.

ART. Don't.

JOHN. Me, too.

DAN. Let me say something right here. There's no way in the whole world for John to prove his story to us, and there's no way for us to disprove it! No matter how outrageous we believe it is, and no matter how highly trained we believe we are, we absolutely can't disprove it. Our friend is either a caveman, a liar, or a nut. So while we're thinking about that, why not just go with it? He may jolt us into believing him, we may jolt him into reality.

EDITH. "Believing"?

ART. Whose reality?

GRUBER. So you're caveman?

JOHN. Yes. I am, or was, a Cro Magnon. I think.

GRUBER. You don't know if you're a caveman or not?

JOHN. Oh, I'm sure about that.

GRUBER. A Cro Magnon, then. When did you first realize this?

JOHN. When the Cro Magnon was first identified. When anthropology gave them a name, I had mine.

GRUBER. Well, please continue. I'm sure you must have more to say.

JOHN. Want me to lie down on the couch?

GRUBER. *(smiles)* As you wish.

> *(Brief silence. GRUBER sips his whiskey.)*

As a physician, I am curious. In the enormous lifetime you describe, have you ever been ill?

JOHN. Sure. As much as anyone else.

GRUBER. Seriously ill?

JOHN. Sometimes.

GRUBER. Of what, do you know?

JOHN. In prehistory, I can't tell you. Maybe pneumonia, once or twice. The last few hundred years, I've gotten over typhoid, yellow fever, smallpox. I survived the black plague.

GRUBER. Bubonic. Terrible.

JOHN. More so than history describes.

GRUBER. And smallpox. You are not scarred.

JOHN. I don't scar.

HARRY. That's not possible!

GRUBER. Let us take John's story at face value, and explore it from that perspective. If he doesn't scar, it's no stranger than the rest of it.

HARRY. Would you come to my lab, John, before you take off? Suffer a few tests from your friendly biologist?

JOHN. No, I'm leery of labs. I could go in and maybe stay in, for a thousand years, while cigarette-smoking men tried to figure me out.

HARRY. You don't think I'd betray you in any way.

JOHN. Walls have ears.

DAN. Medical tests might be a way of proving what you say.

JOHN. I don't *want* to prove it.

ART. You're telling us all this, the yarn of the century, and you don't care if we believe you?

JOHN. I guess I shouldn't have expected you to. You're not as crazy as you think I am.

EDITH. Amen.

SANDY. *(to* **EDITH***)* I've always liked you.

EDITH. Why, thank you, dear...

SANDY. That's changing.

EDITH. Surely you don't believe this nonsense?

SANDY. I think we should remain courteous to someone we've known and trusted.

LINDA. Here you sit – scholars, and you can't break his story. All you can do is thumb your nose at it.

ART. Are you doing that to *us*, John? Laughing at us, inside?

JOHN. I wish you didn't feel that way.

ART. What you're telling us, it offends common sense.

JOHN. So does relativity, quantum mechanics, but that's the way Nature works.

DAN. Your story doesn't fit into Nature as we know it.

JOHN. And we know so little, Dan. Learning all the time. Even experts...each of you probably knows five "geniuses" in your specialty you disagree with; probably one you'd like to strangle.

DAN. I'd strangle all of 'em!

EDITH. Dammit Dan – it's bad enough we have to listen to Harry's idiotic jokes –

HARRY. Well, thank you very much. Maybe when *I* get to be a hundred-ten I'll be as smart as you are.

EDITH. If you lived as long as John, you still wouldn't grow up.

DAN. Aw, take it easy. How often do you meet someone who thinks he is a Stone Age man?

EDITH. Once is enough.

HARRY. Edith?

(She looks up, eyebrow raised. He blows her a kiss. She shakes her head...but her anger dissipates a little.)

DAN. *(beat)* Alright then. A guy with your mind, you would have studied a great deal.

JOHN. I have ten degrees, including all of yours. Except yours, Will.

HARRY. That makes me feel a trifle Lilliputian.

JOHN. But that's over the span of a hundred and seventy years! I got my biology degree at Oxford in 1840, so I'm a little behind the times. The same in other areas. I can't keep up with all the new stuff that comes along. Hell, these days no one can, even in your specialty.

ART. So much for the myth of the super-wise, all knowing immortal.

DAN. I see your point, John. No matter how long a man lives, he can't be in advance of his times. He can't know more than the best of the race knows, if that. When the world learned it was round, you learned it.

JOHN. It took some time. News traveled slowly before communications got fancy. And there were problems of preconception, social obstacles, screams from the church.

ART. Ten Doctorates. Impressive. Have you taught them, John?

JOHN. Some. Look, you all might have done the same. Living fourteen thousand years didn't make me a genius. I just had the time.

DAN. *(pondering)* Time…

(A moment goes by. Everyone looking at DAN. *He notices:)*

DAN *(cont'd)* Oh. You can't see it, hear it, weigh it, you can't isolate it in a laboratory. It's our subjective sense of becoming – becoming what we are – instead of what we were a nanosecond ago – becoming what we will be in another nanosecond. The Hopi see time as a landscape, existing before and behind us. We move through it slice by slice.

LINDA. Clocks measure time.

DAN. They measure themselves. The only objective referent of a clock is another one.

EDITH. Very interesting. What has it to do with John?

DAN. I wonder if he, somehow, exists outside of time, as we know it.

*(*GRUBER *has his hand in his jacket pocket. Speaks up suddenly:)*

GRUBER. People do go around armed these days. *(as all react)* If I shot you, John, you are immortal? Would you survive this?

JOHN. I never said I was immortal, only that I'm old. I might die, and you could wonder the rest of your incarcerated life what it was you killed.

*(*GRUBER *fishes around, takes a pipe from his pocket.)*

GRUBER. May I?

(Relieved expressions. **JOHN** *nods.* **GRUBER** *lights up.)*

HARRY. Preferable to a gun, anyhow.

DAN. That was a little much, Will.

(Brief silence. **GRUBER** *glances at the last box by the door. Books.)*

GRUBER. Books, Doctorates. Yes, you've grown and changed, but there is always innate nature. Wouldn't you be more comfortable squatting in the back yard?

(Several startled looks at **GRUBER**. **DAN**'*s expression says, "What the hell?")*

SANDY. That's a nasty thing to say!

JOHN. Sometimes I do, Will. I look up at the stars and wonder.

GRUBER. What did primitive man make of them?

JOHN. A great mystery. There were gods up there then. Shamans who knew about them told us so.

HARRY. They still do.

GRUBER. Have you ever wished it would end?

JOHN. *(beat)* No.

GRUBER. Fourteen thousand years. Injuries, illness, disasters, you survived them all. You're a very lucky man.

(Silence. **JOHN** *considering Gruber's last line. A sound is heard. A truck pulling up outside.* **JOHN** *goes to the door and opens it, revealing a* **MOVING MAN**.*)*

MOVING MAN #1. John Oldman?

JOHN. Yes.

MOVING MAN #1. Charity Now. We're here to pick up the furniture.

*(**JOHN** *steps aside. The* **MOVING MAN** *enters, followed by another* **MOVING MAN**.*)*

JOHN. It's all yours.

(An awkward moment as the group realizes they'll have to leave their seats. They all rise.)

MOVING MAN #2. *(to* **SANDY***)* Sorry, miss.

SANDY. That's all right.

> (**MOVING MAN #2** *picks up* **SANDY***'s chair, heads for the door. Under following, the two movers are back and forth, in and out, carrying chairs, tables, lamps, etc., to their truck.)*

> (**DAN** *is staring at* **JOHN***.)*

DAN. You're donating it? Everything?

JOHN. I'll get more.

EDITH. Do you always travel this light?

JOHN. Only way to move.

> (*A brief silence, as all realize just how completely* **JOHN** *is severing his ties. Nothing to weigh him down. Finally:)*

GRUBER. *(to* **JOHN***)* You've talked a good deal about your extraordinary amount of living. What do you think of dying, John? Do you fear death?

JOHN. Who wouldn't?

GRUBER. How did primitive man regard death?

JOHN. We had the practical concept. You stopped. You fell down, didn't get up, started to smell bad and come apart. Injuries we could understand. If somebody's insides were all over the ground. Infections were mysterious, aging was the greatest mystery of all.

GRUBER. You realized you were different.

JOHN. Much longer to realize *how* I was different, to synthesize my experience into a view of myself. I even thought for a while there was something wrong with everybody else! They got old and died. So did animals. But not me.

> (**THE MOVING MEN** *are carrying out the box-spring. One gives the other a look. They move on, deadpan.* **LINDA** *is looking at Gruber's pipe, not happily. She coughs.* **GRUBER** *notices.)*

GRUBER. Ah, forgive me, my dear.

> (**GRUBER** *moves toward the front door, opens it.)*

GRUBER *(cont'd) (to* **JOHN***)* You live simply.

(**GRUBER** *moves onto the porch a bit.* **JOHN** *moves to follow him outside.*)

JOHN. I've owned castles. When you're always leaving, why leave a lot? I have money...

HARRY. Got into Microsoft at fifty cents?

(**JOHN** *smiles, and steps outside.* **GRUBER** *looks at John's yard. Scrub and cacti, green-brown hillocks beyond. Now* **GRUBER** *must move aside, as the moving men return for more. During following, he will move out of their way several times.*)

GRUBER. As one grows older, the days, weeks, months go by more quickly. What does a day or a year or a century mean to you? The birth-death cycle.

(**JOHN** *looks past* **GRUBER***, eyes distant.*)

JOHN. Turbulence. I meet people, learn a name, say a word, and they're gone. Others come, like waves, rising and falling. Like ripples in a wheat-field, blown by the wind.

(*Brief silence.*)

GRUBER. Do you ever get tired of it all?

JOHN. I get bored now and then. They make the same stupid mistakes, again and again.

GRUBER. "They?" Then you see yourself as separate from the rest of humanity?

JOHN. I didn't mean it that way! But, of course, I am.

GRUBER. Are you comfortable knowing that you have lived, while everyone you knew – *everyone* you knew, John – has died?

JOHN. I've regretted losing people. Often.

GRUBER. Have you ever felt guilt about that? Something akin to survivors' guilt?

JOHN. I suppose I have, in strict psychological terms. Yes, I have. What could I do about it?

GRUBER. Indeed.

(*For the first time,* **JOHN** *is dark. There have been reactions from our group. Some not liking the tack* **GRUBER** *has taken.*)

(*The movers start to pick up the couch.*)

JOHN. (*to the movers*) Hold on, think I'll keep the couch.

(**THE MEN** *shrug, not caring one way or the other, and begin taking down drapes.* **JOHN** *indicates the couch.*)

JOHN (*cont'd*) Ladies? You, too, Will, and don't grump about it. You have a heart problem.

(**GRUBER** *knocks out his pipe on a porch-post, comes back inside.* **EDITH, SANDY, LINDA** *are on the couch.* **GRUBER** *joins them.* **ART** *squats on the floor.* **DAN** *and* **HARRY** *stand about.* **JOHN** *leans against a wall by the door.*)

HARRY. Could we get away from dying?

GRUBER. But this is the flip side of his coin, Harry. I'm very curious to know his feelings. Would you prefer I asked him about his father?

JOHN. I thought you always started with, "Tell me about your mother."

GRUBER. But prehistory was strongly patriarchal. Certainly you remember your father?

JOHN. I'm not sure. There's a figure I remember, but he may have been an older brother, a social father.

GRUBER. No matter. I can scarcely remember mine.

(**JOHN** *is silent for a moment. Looking off at nothing, at memories past.*)

GRUBER (*cont'd*) Do you feel that as a vacancy in your life, John? Something you wish could be filled by a face, a voice, an image?

JOHN. Not at this late date.

GRUBER. There must be someone, probably many, that you valued intensely. Loved. You saw them age and die. A friend, colleague, a wife? Certainly you have had wives. And children.

(**SANDY** *reacts.*)

JOHN. I'd move on. I had to move on.

HARRY. Making him history's biggest bigamist?

GRUBER. Have you ever in your life thought, "It should have been me?"

JOHN. *(beat)* Maybe.

GRUBER. Art has told me that your early fellows feared you were stealing their lives. *(off John's nod)* Have you thought that perhaps you were, perhaps you are? There have always been legends of such a thing. Creatures, not quite human, taking not blood but the force of life itself.

DAN. My God, Will.

GRUBER. Unconsciously, perhaps, by some biological or psychic mechanism we might only guess at. I'm not saying you would do such a thing deliberately. I'm not saying you would even know how to. Would you?

(The others definitely don't like what's going on. **DAN***, especially.)*

GRUBER *(cont'd)* Would such a thing be fair?

JOHN. You believe me, then?

GRUBER. I am exploring what you have said. Whether I believe or not is of no importance. We will die, you will live? Will you come to my funeral, John?

DAN. Will!

SANDY. You've gone too far. John didn't ask to be what he is.

GRUBER. And we did not ask to hear about it. If it were true, is there one of us who would not feel envy? Even, somewhere, a touch of hatred? You've told us of yourself, John. Can you imagine how we feel?

JOHN. I never thought of that.

GRUBER. Since you may not die, while we assuredly will, there must be a reason for that, no? Perhaps you are an expert.

(**MOVING MAN #1** *pauses at the door, carrying an end-table.*)

MAN 1. That's it, Mr. Oldman. Have a good one.

JOHN. Thanks. You too.

(**THE MOVING MEN** *leave, looking a little relieved. During remainder of the play, we now and then detect the distinctive echo of an empty house.*)

GRUBER. Are you a vampire, John? Even an unknowing one? Do you stand, alive and tall, in a graveyard you helped to fill?

DAN. *(hard)* That's going too far!

GRUBER. Bored? Perhaps lonely, because your heart cannot keep its treasures. Is that your doing? Have you had a wrongful life? Perhaps it is time to die.

(*His hand, having moved back to his pocket, he now quickly draws out an old revolver.* **GRUBER** *aims it at* **JOHN,** *unsteadily.*)

(**DAN** *takes a quick, angry step. Then a more deliberate one, to stand over* **GRUBER.**)

DAN. I don't know what John is doing, but I sure as hell don't like what you're doing! Knock it off, or I'll break your Goddamn arm!

GRUBER. Ah, Dan, you sound like our football coach.

(**GRUBER** *rises, still shakily aiming the pistol at* **JOHN.**)

GRUBER. *(rising)* What do you think, John? A shot to the arm, perhaps we can watch it heal. A bullet in the head...what exactly would happen?

(**JOHN** *holds his gaze at* **GRUBER,** *utterly calm, immobile.* **DAN** *shifts his weight between his feet, deciding when to make his move –*)

(*Suddenly* **GRUBER**'*s arm drops.*)

GRUBER *(cont'd)* I have papers to correct. Much as I dislike the job, it will be preferable to this. I leave you with it.

(**GRUBER** *brushes past* **JOHN,** *out the front door,*

dropping the gun in the dirt. **JOHN** *looks after him, then closes the door. Moment of silence.)*

DAN. Jesus Christ…

(*to* **JOHN**)

What the hell was *that?*

EDITH. Where'd he get a gun?

ART. He had you on the ropes. Are you really so damned smart?

EDITH. That's not like Will…

HARRY. Mary passed away yesterday.

LINDA. Who?

HARRY. His wife. She had pancreatic cancer. *(As others react:)* He didn't want anybody to know.

(**JOHN** *rushes out the front door; catches up to* **GRUBER** *in the yard.)*

JOHN. Will, I didn't know. About Mary. I can see how this might have hit you.

GRUBER. Permit me to be infantile by myself.

(**GRUBER** *shuffles off.* **JOHN** *looks after him.)*

(*He starts back toward the house… bends to pick up the gun. He cracks open the cylinder: the revolver is unloaded.)*

(*While* **JOHN** *is still outside:* **HARRY** *turns angrily on* **ART**.)

HARRY. What the hell were you thinking?

ART. Something had to be done.

EDITH. I have to say I agree.

(**ART** *abandons his squatting position to stretch his legs.)*

ART. Oh, boy. I'm not as young as I used to be.

EDITH. *He* is.

DAN. And he's our friend. Whatever on earth is going on, he's our friend.

EDITH. You're sure about that?

HARRY. Why are you being so hard on him, Edith?

EDITH. One of my favorite people has disappeared. Can you get Alzheimer's at thirty-five? Maybe I'm trying to wake him up. Maybe I'm too sad to cry.

(There's a long beat. They're have nothing to say to each other.)

(JOHN enters, looking regretful.)

JOHN. What I've said about myself – hurt him. He struck back.

DAN. Expertly. That stuff about stealing life force…

JOHN. I've always wondered about the reason.

(Long uncomfortable beat.)

HARRY. We still have an afternoon to pass. Hey, maybe charades? Sandy, c'mere –

(HARRY grabs SANDY; he picks up a fireplace log and makes the wolf whistle sound. He swings the "club" to hit SANDY on the head. Then he grabs her and they plop onto the floor. He looks up expectantly.)

JOHN. *(smiles)* My first wedding.

(Some laughter at that.)

HARRY. And chances are at least one of us is a direct descendant.

(Uncertain laughter.)

DAN. And I didn't send you a Christmas card.

HARRY. What would you send him for a birthday card? And don't get me started on the candles…

(A little laughter. But JOHN is still down, after Gruber's attack. Our group knows this, and tacitly lightens up.)

DAN. I'd like to hear more.

HARRY. Me, too.

LINDA. More.

HARRY. Do you double-damn swear this isn't some story

you're trying out on us?

JOHN. Next question.

ART. You realize this is an invitation to the men in white with the happy pills?

DAN. *(thoughtful)* If it was true – a mechanism enabling survival for thousands of years...

ART. We'd run out of room even faster.

DAN. Then one day you might live on Mars. A colony, as we expand. As we'll have to.

JOHN. I'd like that. Later, on a planet of another star.

DAN. I'd envy you.

LINDA. Did you have a pet dinosaur?

(A chuckle or two.)

JOHN. They were quite a bit before my time.

DAN. I'm glad something is.

ART. No doubt you could give us a thousand details, John, corroborating your story. From La Madeleine to the Buddha, to now.

JOHN. Ten thousand. And you could say, out of the books.

EDITH. It's getting chilly.

(JOHN throws another log on the fire. Looks a moment at the swirling sparks, face somber, and turns away.)

DAN. Now here's a question...*(as they look at him)* Could there be others like you, John? Who escaped aging as you have?

HARRY. Representing something terrific we don't know about biology.

DAN. Learning all the time.

HARRY. How would he know? He doesn't wear an I.D. badge or armband, saying "yabba-dabba-doo."

JOHN. There was one time. In the early 1600's, I met a man –

EDITH. *(suddenly cuts in)* Where were you in 1292 A.D.?

JOHN. Where were you a year ago on this date?*(as Edith retreats)* I met a man, and had a hunch he was – like me. So much so that I told him.

ART. You said this was a first.

JOHN. I forgot.

DAN. A crack in your story, John?

JOHN. A touch of senility. Anyway, he said yes, he was, but from another time, another place. We talked for two days, it was all pretty convincing. But we couldn't be sure. We each said things that the other confirmed, but how could we know if the confirmation was genuine or an echo? I knew I was kosher, but maybe he was playing a game – a scholar of all we talked about. He said he was compelled to the same reservations.

DAN. Now, that's interesting. Just as we could never be sure, even if we wanted to – if we were sure, you couldn't be sure of that.

JOHN. We parted, agreeing to keep in touch. We didn't, of course. Two hundred years later I thought I saw him in a Brussels train station. I lost him in the crowd.

EDITH. Oh, what a shame! I mean, if it was true.

HARRY. How's this for a question? What do you do with your spare time?

(some laughter)

JOHN. Maybe every fifty years or so, when I want to get away from the rush, I go back to a hidden tribe in New Guinea, where I'm revered as an immortal God. There's even a statue of me. I'd show you a photograph, but it's packed.

EDITH. I won't make the obvious nasty crack about more unwashed cavemen.

JOHN. Actually bathing was the style until the Middle Ages, when the church said removing God's dirt was sinful. So they got sewn into their underwear in October and peeled out of it in April.

EDITH. You say you just happened. I don't believe that. If your story's true, why did God allow you to happen?

(Art's expression says: "Ask him.")

DAN. That raises an interesting point. Are you religious, John?

JOHN. Do I follow a known religion? No.

DAN. Ever?

JOHN. A long time ago. Most people do at one time or another. Some just never get over it.

DAN. Do you believe in God?

JOHN. As LaPlace said, "I have no need of that hypothesis." He may be around, though.

EDITH. He's everywhere. You just can't see him.

HARRY. If I couldn't do any better than this, I'd be hiding too.

(As **EDITH** *glares at* **HARRY***:)*

DAN. And Creation?

JOHN. It's here. I'm not so sure it was created.

EDITH. What, then?

JOHN. Maybe it just accumulated, fields affecting fields.

ART. And the source of the field energies? Doesn't that imply a Prime Mover?

JOHN. I'd wonder about the source of the Prime Mover. Infinite regress. It doesn't imply anything to me. Back to the mystery.

EDITH. That's a very old question, but there's no answer except in religious terms. If you have faith, it's answered.

DAN. Did you ever meet any people from our religious history? A biblical figure?

JOHN. *(beat)* In a way.

EDITH. Who?

JOHN. We'd better skip this one.

HARRY. Oh, come on, John, we're curious!

JOHN. Next question.

GROUP. *(a chorus)* No skipping! Come on, John! Tell us! We want to know! Don't do this to us! *(etc.)*

(As the chorus subsides, DAN *is looking thoughtfully at* JOHN:)

DAN. Good Lord, *were* you one of them?

(Big reaction from JOHN, *which he tries to conceal.)*

JOHN. This isn't going where I thought it would, or hoped it would. We should call it a night.

ART. My ass. Spit this one out if you would, John. You were someone in religious history?

JOHN. *(beat)* Yes.

EDITH. In the bible?

JOHN. Yes.

HARRY. Someone we know?

EDITH. How could we not know someone in the bible?

HARRY. I meant somebody important.

JOHN. You may think you know him. Most of it's myth.

ART. Well, for Pete's sake, the whole bible is myth and allegory, but maybe with some basis in historical events. You're saying you were part of that history.

JOHN. Yes.

LINDA. Moses.

JOHN. Moses was modeled on Mises, from Assyrian myth. There are earlier versions. All found floating on water, a staff that turned into a snake, the parting of waters to lead followers to freedom. Even received laws on stone or wooden tablets.

LINDA. One of the Apostles.

JOHN. They weren't Apostles. I mean, they didn't do any teaching, that I know of. They were students. Paul the Fisherman learned some new things about fishing.

ART. How would you know that?

(Silence.)

JOHN. The mystical overlay is enormous, and not a good thing. The truth of it's so simple. So simple. The new New Testament in a hundred words or less. Are you ready for it?

(**EDITH** *stands up.*)

EDITH. I don't think I want to hear this. Harry, will you take me home?

HARRY. No. I mean, not right now. I want to hear this.

ART. Sit down, Edith, you're acting as if you believed him.

EDITH. It's sacrilege.

HARRY. How can it be sacrilege when he hasn't said anything yet?

EDITH. The "new" New Testament is sacrilege.

(**JOHN** *gets up and moves across the room, as if to get away from the conflict.*)

DAN. There have been a *dozen* new New Testaments, from Hebrew to Greek to Latin to Tyndale, all the way to King James. All revisionist and all called "revealed truth."

EDITH. I mean a new New Testament in a hundred words.

HARRY. How about the Ten Commandments in ten words? "Don't, don't, don't... "

DAN. The Commandments are just updates of more ancient laws...Hammurabi's Code –

HARRY. And they weren't even the first. I was raised on the Torah, my wife on the Koran. My oldest son is an atheist, my youngest's a Scientologist, and my daughter is studying Hinduism. I suppose there's room for a holy war in my living room, but we live and let live.

(*to* **EDITH**:)

What's your preferred version of the bible?

EDITH. The King James, of course. It's the most modern, the work of great scholars.

DAN. Modern is good?

(*As* **EDITH** *glares:*)

HARRY. Okay, John, get on with the short form.

JOHN. A guy met the Buddha, and liked what he heard. He

thought about it for a while, say, five-hundred years, while he returned to the Mediterranean, became an Etruscan, and then seeped into the Roman Empire. He didn't like what they became. A giant killing machine. He went to the Near East, thinking "Why not pass the Buddha's teachings along in modern form?" So he tried. One dissident against Rome, Rome won. The rest is history, sort of. A lot of fairy tales mixed in.

(Silence. Staring faces. Finally:)

EDITH. I knew it. He's saying he was Christ.

JOHN. Oh, no. That's the medal they pinned on Jesus, to fulfill prophecy.

DAN. The crucifixion?

JOHN. He blocked the pain. He'd learned to do that in India and Tibet. To slow body processes to the point where they weren't detectable. After a while he did that, so they thought he was dead. His followers put him in a cave. His body normalized, as he'd told it to. He tried to get away undetected, but some devotees were standing watch. He tried to explain what had happened, but they were in ecstasy.

(beat)

So I was resurrected. I ascended to central Europe, to get as far away as I could.

EDITH. You don't mean a word of this, John! My God, why are you doing this?

ART. Let me see your wrists.

JOHN. I don't scar. Besides, they tied me. But nails and blood make better religious art.

HARRY. All the speculations about Jesus. He was black, he was Asian, he was a blue-eyed Aryan with gold beard and hair just out of Vidal Sassoon's, he was a benevolent alien, he never existed at all. Now he's a caveman.

DAN. The Christ figure goes back to Krishna. And Hercules, of course.

HARRY. Hercules?

JOHN. Born of a virgin, Alcmene. A god for a father, Zeus. The only begotten, called Savior, the Greek Soter – the Good Shepherd, Nuelos Emelos – the Prince of Peace, bringing divine wisdom and gentle persuasion. He died and joined his father on Olympus. A thousand years before Gethsemane.

EDITH. How can you compare pagan mythology to the true Word!

HARRY. Pretty closely, I'd say.

DAN. The early Christian priests threw away Hebrew manuscripts, and borrowed from pagan sources all over the place.

EDITH. Do you realize how – inconsiderately – you're treating my feelings?

DAN. About as inconsiderately as we've treated John's?

EDITH. He doesn't believe what he's saying!

SANDY. Do you believe, literally, every word in the bible?

EDITH. Yes. Before you say it. I know it's undergone a lot of changes, but God has spoken through Man to make his word clearer.

HARRY. He couldn't get it right the first time?

EDITH. We're imperfect! He had to work to make us understand.

HARRY. He couldn't get us right the first time?

DAN. *(to* **EDITH,** *at first:)* Taken alone, the philosophical teachings attributed to Jesus are Buddhism with a Hebrew accent. Kindness, tolerance, brotherhood, love, and a ruthless realism acknowledging that life is as it is. Here and now. The Kingdom of God, meaning goodness, is on Earth. Or should be. That's where the Buddha brought it.

JOHN. And that's what I taught, but a snake made a lady eat an apple, so we're screwed. Heaven and Hell were peddled so priests could rule through seduction and terror, so they could save our souls that we never lost in the first place. Hope is a bargain at any price. I threw a clean pass, and they ran it out of the ballpark.

EDITH. This is blasphemy! It's horrible! Who else were you? Solomon? Elvis? Jack the Ripper?

DAN. It's been said that Jesus and the Buddha would laugh or cry if they knew what's been done in their names.

HARRY. If there is a Creator, maybe he feels the same way.

JOHN. I see rituals. Candles, processions, genuflecting, moaning, intoning, sprinkling water, venerating cookies and wine, and I think, "This isn't what I had in mind"

EDITH. That's Vatican flapdoodle! It doesn't have a thing to do with God!

DAN. As you said, John, everywhere religions. From exalting life to purging joy as a sin. Rome does it as grand opera. But the same old pessimism – the path of simple goodness needs a supernatural roadmap.

HARRY. Supernatural!

ART. Stupid word. Anything that happens, happens within Nature. Whether we understand it or not.

JOHN. Like a fourteen-thousand-year old caveman?

(*We hear the sound of a car pulling up outside.* **JOHN** *goes to the door. Opens it before* **GRUBER** *can ring.*)

(*Outside, evening has arrived, with the pastel lavender and gold of the desert sunset. The breeze has become steady.*)

GRUBER. I drove for a while, and then sat for a while. I – am ashamed. And I'm freezing.

(**JOHN** *steps back.* **GRUBER** *enters.*)

GRUBER (*cont'd*) I still don't believe you, of course. You need help.

JOHN. Everybody needs help.

(**JOHN** *briefly embraces* **GRUBER** *'s shoulders, as* **GRUBER** *nods to the group and moves to hug the fire.*)

ART. Now he's Jesus.

HARRY. As in, you know, Mr. Jesus H. Christ. Himself.

(**GRUBER** *is thinking over what he's been told.*)

GRUBER. From the Buddha to the cross. I have always regarded both as entirely mythic. I would like to hear more. May I lie a moment on the couch? I am not as young as I used to be.

(*Some eyes go to* **EDITH.** *She is silent.* **LINDA** *and* **SANDY** *get up, to curl on the floor.* **EDITH** *moves over to give* **GRUBER** *room. He sits down, swings to lie down. Pulls up a blanket.*)

GRUBER *(cont'd)* So. You were Jesus. Well, perhaps somebody had to be, for better or worse. The jury is still out. And when did you begin to believe you were Jesus?

JOHN. When did you begin to believe you were a psychiatrist?

GRUBER. Since I graduated Harvard Medical School and finished my residency, I have had that feeling. I sometimes dream about it.

JOHN. Have you acted upon this belief?

GRUBER. I had a private practice for a while. Then I taught. Nothing unusual, until one day I met a caveman who thought he was Jesus.

JOHN. Do you find that unusual?

GRUBER. Very. I would stake my reputation that he is as sane as I am. Why does he persist in such a story?

JOHN. There must be a reason for that, no?

GRUBER. Unless I have imagined it all. Is that possible?

JOHN. I think you're as sane as he is.

GRUBER. Oh, God, no!

(*They both chuckle.*)

Did you ever find it prudent to worship yourself, rather than be thought a heretic? That would be something.

ART. Hilarious.

JOHN. Other times Christianity was heresy. I had to pretend other faiths.

GRUBER. And what does Jesus have to say to those present, who find it difficult to believe in him?

JOHN. Believe in what he tried to teach. Without rigmarole. Piety is not what the lessons bring to people, it's a mistake they bring to the lessons.

(JOHN *glances out the window.*)

Getting to be night. Stuff to carry. I've got a long drive.

SANDY. I'll help.

DAN. You have a destination, John? Never mind, I won't ask.

(JOHN *and* SANDY *bring out the last two boxes of books. They carry them out the front door towards the truck.*)

(*The room is in half-darkness. Some have put on jackets again.*)

GRUBER. Anyone, mentally ill, can imagine a fantastic background, an entire life, and sincerely believe it. The man who thinks he is Napoleon does believe it. His true identity has taken a back seat to his delusion, and the need for it. If that is the case with John, there is a grave disorder.

ART. Organized brilliantly. He's got an answer for everything.

GRUBER. It might involve a rejection of his father, of his entire early past, replaced by this fantasy.

HARRY. He says he can't remember his father.

GRUBER. Precisely. Why?

LINDA. You said you thought he was sane.

GRUBER. Did I?

DAN. Could our caveman have a monkey on his back?

EDITH. Drugs? Oh, my, I hadn't thought of that.

HARRY. I've done consulting work for the Narcotics Division. I've seen a lot of people tripping. Whatever gives with John, I don't think it's that. I've looked for signs. Not one.

LINDA. Could cavemen really talk?

(**EDITH** *rolls her eyes impatiently.*)

DAN. We think language came into existence maybe sixty thousand years ago. The structure of Stone Age cultures is evidence of the ability to communicate verbally.

HARRY. *(indicating Linda)* [he wolf-whistles].

ART. Oh, shut up.

(*The people inside the cabin continue to speak but we don't hear them. Shift our attention outside –* **JOHN** *puts the last box in the station-wagon. He turns to go back inside, and* **SANDY** *puts a hand on his arm.*)

JOHN. Maybe it'd be easier if I *were* just –

SANDY. *(cutting in)* Crazy?

(*shakes her head – soft*)

No.

(*They share a moment of silence, under the beautiful nighttime sky. Each wanting to say more, but knowing there's no need.*)

(**JOHN** *looks off, hearing something she doesn't. A moment later, we hear the Howl of a distant coyote.*)

(**SANDY** *returns her gaze to* **JOHN**, *and sees that he's looking at her, with an expression of deep fondness. And beneath that, she sees a loneliness in his eyes, that she cannot begin to comprehend.* **JOHN** *smiles softly. She smiles back.*)

(*Back inside the house…each with their own thoughts. Finally:*)

DAN. It is fascinating. A brave attempt to teach Buddhism in the west. It's no wonder he failed, we're not ready for it.

EDITH. Now you're talking as if you believed him.

DAN. Well, it's possible, isn't it? Anything is possible!

(*off* **EDITH**'s *defiant glare*)

We have two simple choices. We can get all bent out of shape – intellectualizing, bench-pressing logic – or we can relax and enjoy it. I can listen critically, but I don't have to make up my mind about anything! Do you think you do?

ART. Unfortunately, there aren't any authorities on prehistory. We couldn't stop him on that.

EDITH. There are experts on the bible!

HARRY. Dream on.

DAN. Thus the "lost years" of Jesus. They didn't exist, because *He* didn't, until John put on the hat.

EDITH. I don't believe about angels and the Nativity and a star in the East, but there are stories about the childhood of Jesus.

(During following, LINDA moves to sit on the floor near the fireplace. ART thinks about it for a moment. Then joins her.)

GRUBER. History hates a vacuum. Improvisation, even sincere, will fill in the gaps. It would have been easy to falsify a past then. A few words, credulity and time would do the rest.

EDITH. Now *you're* talking as if you believed him!

ART. Look at the popular myths about the Kennedy assassination, in just a few short years. Conspiracy, Mafia, CIA – a mystique that will never go away.

DAN. It's always been a small step, from a fallen leader to a god.

(DAN has joined those by the fireplace. Squatting, holding hands near the flames. He sits.)

EDITH. Nobody will deify Kennedy! I think we're more sophisticated than that.

DAN. We are? We are...

(JOHN and SANDY enter.)

HARRY. Well, you're finally fulfilling one prophecy about the millennium, John.

JOHN. What's that?

HARRY. Here you are again!

*(No one laughs. **JOHN** closes a window the last inch, and kneels to place another log on the fire. It flares up, filling the room with flickering shadows, quickly dies down again. **JOHN** remains kneeling. Others sitting nearby look at him.)*

(More and more there is the sense of time and place falling away. They could be hunters sitting around a campfire, sharing tales of the day.)

GRUBER. You like the fire, John.

JOHN. Everywhere I've lived, I've had a fireplace. A childhood fixation, I suppose. I feel insecure without it.

SANDY. There are predators out there.

*(**SANDY** moves to sit beside **JOHN** at the fireplace. Leans her head against his shoulder.)*

JOHN. One last thing I didn't pack. Thought I might need it.

(He reaches over to turn on a midget CD-player beside the fireplace. The 2nd movement of Beethoven's Seventh, low volume.)

ART. Wouldn't "Sacre du Printemps" be more appropriate?

HARRY. *(to **ART**)* What?

DAN. *(to **JOHN**)* You have four men of science totally baffled, my friend. We don't know what to make of you.

JOHN. Did you know Voltaire was the first to suggest that the universe originated in a gigantic explosion? Not that he was right, according to Paul. And Goethe was the first to suggest that spiral nebulae were swirling masses of stars, which we now call galaxies. Funny how new concepts in science sometimes find first tentative expression in the arts.

*(Now **HARRY** and **EDITH** are moving to join those sitting by the fire. **GRUBER** remains stolidly on the couch, blanket over lap and legs.)*

HARRY. *(sitting down)* So did Beethoven do physics on the side?

SANDY. He spent most of his time lying on the floor in front of his legless piano, surrounded by orange peels and apple cores.

HARRY. We're on the floor, listening to Beethoven. Full circle.

DAN. You don't have any religious beliefs? Or you haven't given it much thought?

JOHN. You don't get there by thought.

DAN. You have faith?

JOHN. In a lot of things.

SANDY. Do you have faith in the future of the race?

JOHN. I've seen species come and go. It depended on their balance with the environment.

DAN. We've made a mess of it.

JOHN. There's time. If we use it right.

EDITH. Christianity's been a worldwide belief for two thousand years.

JOHN. How long did the Egyptians worship Isis? The Sumerians, Ishtar? Sacred cows wander freely in parts of India, as reincarnated souls. In a few thousand years they'll be barbecued, and the souls will be in squirrels.

EDITH. You weren't Jesus.

(The room is getting darker. Outside, the breeze has turned to steady light wind. Somewhere something rattles, then is silent.)

SANDY. If it rains, you'd better –

JOHN. It's not going to rain.

ART. How do you know?

JOHN. I don't smell it.

LINDA. Were you ever, I guess, a medicine man?

JOHN. I was shaman a few times. I've revealed a lot of truths, in order to eat better.

EDITH. You think that's all religion is about? Selling hope and survival?

JOHN. The Old Testament sells fear and guilt. The New Testament is a great work of ethics, put into my mouth by better philosophers and poets than I am. But the message isn't practiced. The fairy tales build churches.

ART. What about the name "Jesus"? Did you pick it out of a hat?

JOHN. I called myself John, I almost always do. As tales of the resurrection spread, the name was confused with the Hebrew Yohanan, meaning "God is gracious." My stay on earth was seen as divine proof of immortality. That led to "God is salvation," or in Hebrew, "Yeshua," which in translations became my proper name, changing to the Late Greek Iesous, then to Late Latin Iesus, finally to Medieval Latin Jesus. It was a wonder to watch.

DAN. Then you didn't claim to be the son of God?

JOHN. It began as a schoolhouse and ended as a temple. I said I had a Master, who was greater than myself. I wanted to teach what I had learned. I never said he was my father. I never claimed to be king of the Jews, I didn't walk on water, I didn't raise the dead, I never spoke of the divine except in the sense of human goodness on Earth. No wise men came from the East to worship at a manger. I did do a little healing, employing Eastern medicine I'd learned.

DAN. The Three Wise Men first appeared in a myth about the birth of the Buddha.

HARRY. I should be home, kissing my wife. We're trapped by your story, John, hoping for an outcome, I guess. Are there more revelations to come?

(JOHN *shakes his head, no. Firelight. Tired faces. Now that's all that can be seen, a glowing orange cameo on a matte of darkness. A sense that there's a room out there, or something else, or nothing.* JOHN *stirs the fire with a poker. Looks into it.*)

DAN. Just like old times?

(Silence. A gust of wind. The flames.)

EDITH. You weren't Jesus...

HARRY. Quote the Sermon on the Mount!

JOHN. *(laughs)* Sure. Which version do you want? King James? Darby? New American Standard?

EDITH. Do you know them all?

JOHN. No...My point is no one knows the one. Not even me. I *did* try some teaching one day, from a hill...Not many stayed to listen.

DAN. But you –

JOHN. The biblical Jesus said, "Who do you think I am?" He gave them a choice. I'm giving you one.

EDITH. ...*Were* you?

JOHN. If I said no, could you ever be sure?

(Ten seconds of silence. Only the intermittent wind, the crackle-pop of the fire. Then a sob, in the darkness.
EDITH. *Finally she's crying.* **LINDA** *tries to console her. The sobs grow. Suddenly:)*

(The lights come on, brutally. **GRUBER** *has risen and crossed to the switch on the wall.)*

GRUBER. *(nods at CD-player)* Turn that off, please.

*(**JOHN** does so)*

This has gone far enough. It has gone much too far. These people are very upset. I don't believe you are mad, but what you're saying is not true! That leaves one explanation. The time has come when you must admit this is a hoax, a lie. Isn't that true, John? If you don't stop this now – if you can – I'll be convinced that you need a great deal of attention. I can have you committed for observation. You know that. I ask you now, I demand it, that you tell these people the truth! Give them closure. *(off* **JOHN***'s silence)* It is time. Please.

*(**EDITH** has been crying during above, but less and less as she hears what's being said.)*

(**JOHN** *remains silent for a moment. But his expression, looking around, tells it all.*)

JOHN. End of the line. Everybody off.

(*Slow reactions at first. As if rousing from a dream. Double-takes. Then a flurry of realization.*)

DAN. W-w-w-what?

JOHN. It's a story. I'm sorry, it's only a story.

(*A sudden Deluge of reactions. Total deflation, shock, disgusted impatience, sour humor. A sagging* **EDITH** *bursts out crying again, release from tension.*)

HARRY. Oh, man…

(*During following, more frustrated reactions.* **GRUBER**'s *expression remains one of professional scrutiny.*)

DAN. (*some relief*) Another fairy tale.

ART. My – God!

EDITH. All of it? But why? What in the name of Heaven made you?

ART. You had us wondering if you were sane, and you call it just a story? Whatever gave you such a half-baked asinine idea!

JOHN. At least you're relieved I'm not a nut?

ART. I might have preferred it.

JOHN. You gave me the idea. All of you.

DAN. Come again?

JOHN. Edith saw my fake van Gogh –

EDITH. You could have just told me!

JOHN. – and commented that I never age, Art gave me his book on early man, you spotted the burin, and said, "If stones could speak."

DAN. I knew it!

JOHN. I got the notion, and ran it past you, to check your reactions. It went too far.

DAN. (*looming over* **JOHN**) "Too far?" Check *my* reaction.

JOHN. And you asked if I was a figure in religious history.

You asked if I created future identities. You asked if there might be another like me. We were chasing our tails around the maypole, enjoying the mystery, the analytical stretch. You were playing my game, I was playing yours.

DAN. Well, you kept us going! I have to admit, you're good! You know those Chinese boxes, one inside the other inside the other? I feel like I'm in the last box. You son of a bitch! How could you do it to us?

EDITH. I was worried about you.

JOHN. I know. I was tempted to cop out a dozen times, but I wanted to see if you could refute what I was saying. I had the perfect audience. An anthropologist, biologist, archeologist, a Christian literalist.

(*We see* SANDY*'s expression, looking at* JOHN.)

ART. Linda, I'm leaving. You coming?

HARRY. (*as* LINDA *rises*) Do you plan to write the story?

JOHN. If I do, I'll send you copies.

ART. You can keep mine. You're a lunatic. I don't know you.

(ART *exits.*)

LINDA. It was nice seeing you again, Dr. Oldman. Your name's a pun, isn't it? Old man. Did it help with your story idea?

ART. (*impatient, from outside*) Linda.

(*She goes out the front door, joins* ART *on the porch, he practically drags her to the motorcycle O.S.*)

JOHN. Well, Art's half right.

HARRY. Which half? (*off* JOHN*'s silence*) At least, I won't have to throw away half of everything I know about biology.

JOHN. Which half?

DAN. It was a beautiful idea, so rich with possibilities.

JOHN. (*to* GRUBER) Maybe you should do a paper on it, doctor?

(We hear the motorcycle start up, pull away.)

GRUBER. Maybe I will interview you in the rubber room, for further details. You may still need help, my friend.

(Various expressions of relief, resentment. Impatience with John, perhaps at their own self-indulgence. Even a touch of disappointment?)

(JOHN quietly starts to gather up refuse. Paper plates, cups, Coke cans. Silence from all...)

(JOHN stuffs refuse into a garbage bag and marches outside with it. SANDY follows quickly. As soon as they are out of earshot:)

SANDY. *(quietly)* My ass.

JOHN. *(as quietly)* I thought it sounded pretty good.

SANDY. They believe you because they have to. You can't destroy their universe. But one thing I know is you would never use people – abuse their good will and intelligence – like they think you've done to them.

JOHN. Psych 101?

SANDY. Woman, one on one. So you're a pretty fast liar. Are you still Mr. Ugh? What is your real name?

JOHN. Believe it or not, the sound was "Jon."

SANDY. Why did you cave to Gruber?

JOHN. What had happened was enough. Not what I wanted, but not surprising.

(She moves closer to look up into his face.)

SANDY. Fourteen thousand years old. I bet that's a lot of women.

JOHN. Are we counting?

(EDITH and HARRY appear on the porch.)

HARRY. I'm taking Edith home. Sandy?

SANDY. I'll stay.

EDITH. Are you sorry for some of those things you said?

JOHN. I'm sorry I said them.

EDITH. Well, like a good Christian. *(gives JOHN a hug)* Oh,

John, you did a terrible thing, but we're so thankful you're all right. Even Art. He just hates things he can't understand.

HARRY. You're a sadist, but I got a kick out of chasing my tail around the maypole, even though that's all I caught. In any case, good luck, John. I do wish you the best.

(As **EDITH** and **HARRY** turn away, **DAN** appears at the door. His face wears a peculiar expression.)

JOHN. Dan?

DAN. I don't know. There's something about this, John. Something about you. The longer I think about it, I'm not in that Chinese box any more. I sense – space. A kind of latitude in what we happily call reality – in which, as everybody keeps saying, anything is possible. (as **JOHN** opens his mouth) Not a word, please. I'm going home and watch "Star Trek" – for a dose of reality. Good luck, wherever all this leads you. Drop me a line, let me know how you're making out.

JOHN. I will.

(They shake warmly. **DAN** leaves. **JOHN** ties garbage bags.)

(Unseen by **JOHN** or **SANDY**, **GRUBER** has moved to the door and can hear them.)

SANDY. So, John Oldman, how many other pun names have you used?

JOHN. Sometimes John Newman. John Savage. John Paley, for Paleolithic. I got a little wild about sixty years ago, teaching at Harvard. I was John Thomas Partee. Boston, Tea-party? Get it?

(**SANDY** laughs.)

GRUBER. (Big reaction) Boston? Sixty years ago? John Partee?

(**GRUBER** wavers in the doorway. Puts out a hand to steady himself.)

GRUBER *(cont'd) (almost violently)* You did not – teach chemistry!

(**JOHN's** *silence is the answer.*)

GRUBER *(cont'd)* I do NOT – believe you!

(**JOHN** *moves to help* **GRUBER**. *Sober understanding.*)

JOHN. Your mother's name was Nora.

GRUBER. *(stricken)* No! Yes, Nora! My mother! I REJECT THIS! I – my – my dog's name? We had him before I was born!

(**JOHN** *thinks for a moment.*)

JOHN. Wolfie.

(**GRUBER** *moans. Lumbers away from the door on wobbly legs, back into the cabin, in no particular direction. An agony of conflicting emotions. He bumps the counter, braces hands on it.* **JOHN** *and* **SANDY** *are on either side of him.*)

JOHN *(cont'd)* The name Gruber. Nora remarried?

GRUBER. She said we were abandoned.

(**GRUBER** *slumps over the counter. He raises his head to peer at* **JOHN**, *not focusing.* **JOHN** *and* **SANDY** *steady him, looking at each other across his bowed shoulders.*)

JOHN. I'm sorry she told you that. I left, as I had to. And I left enough.

GRUBER. I – cold…

JOHN. Little Chilly Willy. You never could stand cold.

GRUBER. You – had a beard.

JOHN. You'd pull it to see if it was real.

(**JOHN** *places a hand on Gruber's arm.* **GRUBER** *clasps it with his other hand.* **GRUBER** *suddenly gasps. Convulses. Stumbles, falls…In a second* **JOHN** *has him on his back, performing chest compression. Stops for a moment to check airway.*)

JOHN *(cont'd) (at* **SANDY***)* 911!

(SANDY *stumbles to the bedroom. We hear her frantic voice, but not the words.*)

JOHN *(cont'd)* C'mon, Will –

(JOHN *continues chest compression, then starts mouth to mouth.*)

(SANDY *returns. Watches from the doorway, crying, as* JOHN *continues futilely, pumping, counting, breathing…*)

(*And then, at last…*JOHN *gives up. Caresses Gruber's brow.*)

JOHN *(cont'd)* Willy…

(JOHN *is on the verge of tears…finally, after all these years, a new experience. Not a good feeling.*)

(SANDY *raises her head to gasp in air. Crying. As she lowers her head,* JOHN *shoots her a look, expression almost fierce. Does she have strength?*)

(*We hear the Siren as an ambulance approaches.*)

(*Lights fade to black; the only illumination is a red emergency beacon flashing across the stage; it fades to black.*)

(*As we fade back up, Gruber's body is gone.* JOHN *and* SANDY *stand in the doorway, watching as a* PARAMEDIC *and a* POLICE OFFICER *quietly converse in the yard. The* PARAMEDIC *exits, and we hear the sound of his ambulance start up and drive off.*)

(*The* OFFICER *approaches* JOHN:)

OFFICER. You'll keep in touch, Dr. Oldman, in case there are any questions?

JOHN. I'll be back for the funeral.

(*The* OFFICER *flips his note-pad shut, tips his hat to* SANDY, *and exits across the yard. We'll hear his car drive away.* JOHN *steps onto the porch. Pauses to look up.*)

(*Icy wind ruffles John's hair, his shirt. He doesn't seem to notice, though* SANDY *is shivering.*)

SANDY. You never saw a grown child die.

(JOHN *is silent. She starts to put a hand on his arm –*)

JOHN. No.

(SANDY *winces back. She watches from the door, miserable but not objecting, as* JOHN *enters the house. He gathers up the CD-player. Turns off the lights, goes outside, and gets in his wagon. Starts it up. But he doesn't drive off just yet.*)

(SANDY *watches from the porch.* JOHN *turns to face her… he smiles, sadly. She smiles, too.*)

(*As* SANDY *goes down the steps to join* JOHN, *the lights slowly fade.*)

The End

PRODUCTION STILLS FROM THE MOTION PICTURE
JEROME BIXBY'S THE MAN FROM EARTH

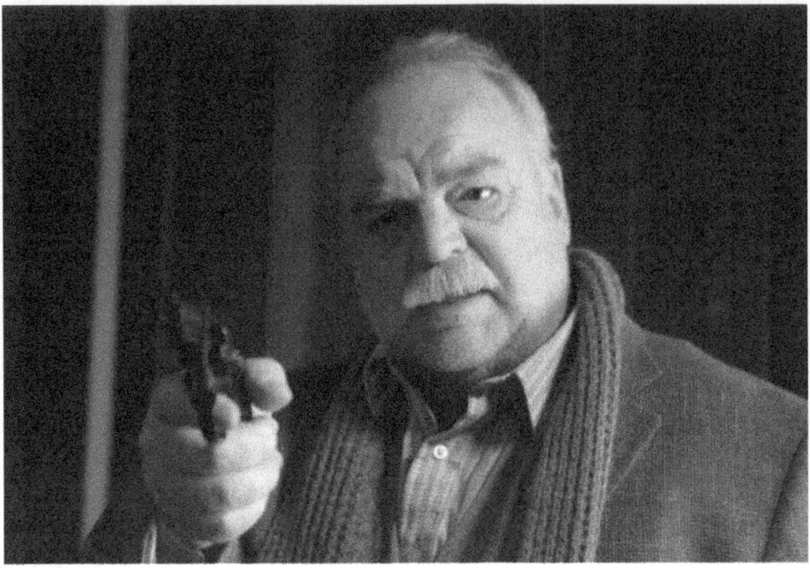

Dr. Gruber (Richard Riehle), the bereaved psychiatrist, makes his point.

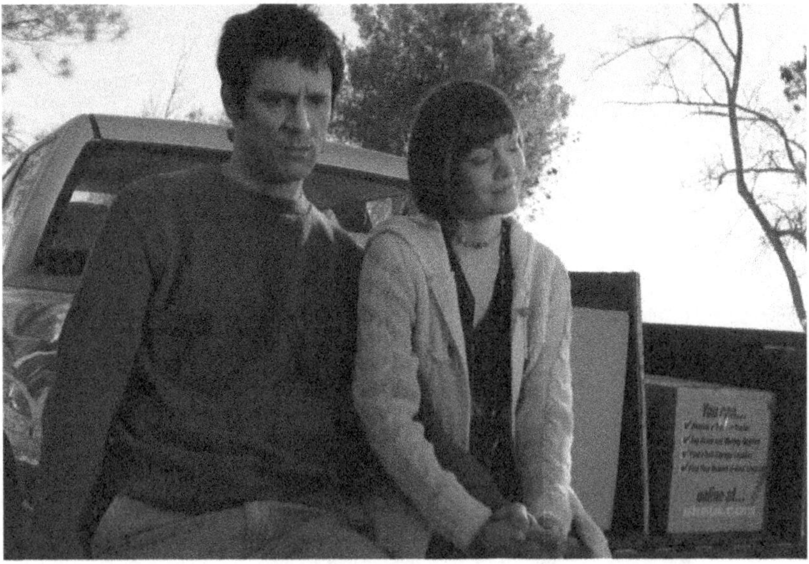

John (David Lee Smith) and Sandy (Annnika Peterson) share a romantic moment.

PRODUCTION STILLS FROM THE MOTION PICTURE
JEROME BIXBY'S THE MAN FROM EARTH

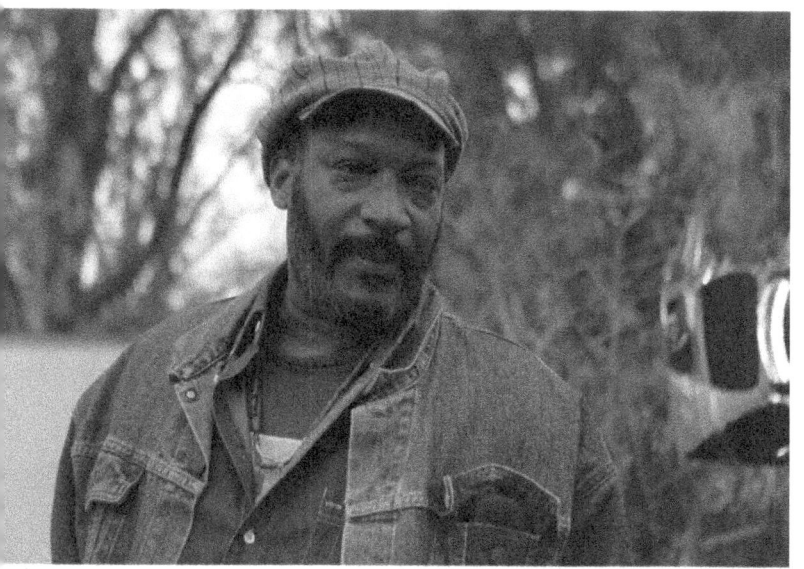

Tony Todd ("Dan", the anthropologist) rehearses off-set.

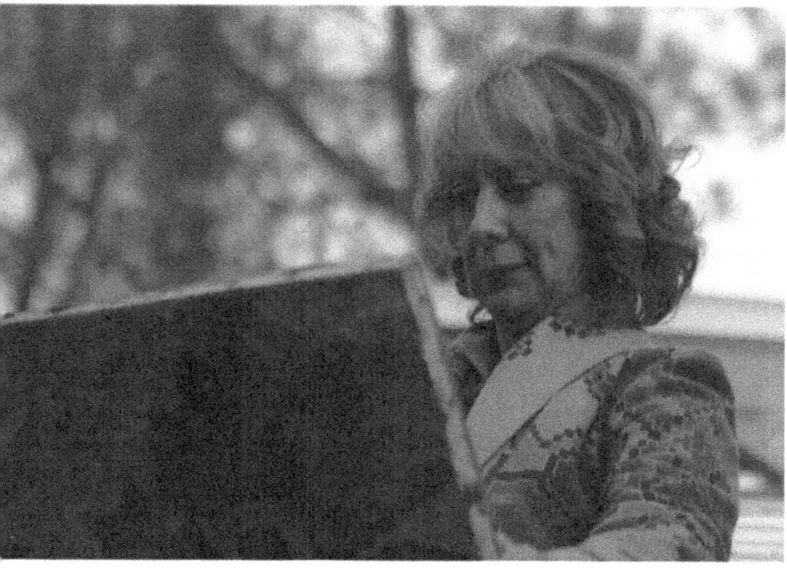

Edith, the art professor (Ellen Crawford) examines John's "Van Gogh".

Printed in August 2021
by Rotomail Italia S.p.A., Vignate (MI) - Italy